First Grade Ladybugs

by Joanne Ryder

Pictures by Betsy Lewin

Troll Associates

To Herb Sandburg,
who nurtures flowers and teachers
in his gardens.
—JR

Library of Congress Cataloging-in-Publication Data

Ryder, Joanne.
First grade ladybugs / by Joanne Ryder; pictures by Betsy Lewin.
p. cm. (First grade is the best!)
Summary: Mrs. Lee's first grade class plants a vegetable and flower garden. Includes instructions for making an indoor garden.
ISBN 0-8167-3006-7 (lib. bdg.) ISBN 0-8167-3007-5 (pbk.)
[1. Gardening—Fiction. 2. Gardens—Fiction. 3. Schools—Fiction.] I. Lewin, Betsy, ill. II. Title. III. Series.
PZ7.R959Fi 1993
[E]—dc20 92-43528

Printed in the United States of America.

10 9 8 7 6 5 4 3 2 1

"Can we go on a field trip?" Robin asked her teacher. "My brother Ben says the fourth graders are going to the park. Can we go to a park like the fourth graders?"

"Not yet, Robin," Mrs. Lee said.

"My brother was right," said Robin. "He said we're too little to do anything."

“That’s not true,” said Mrs. Lee. “We can make a park here in school.”

“With trees?” asked Brian.

“No, but with plenty of plants,” Mrs. Lee said. “I’ve been thinking of starting an outdoor garden.”

The first graders thought this was a fine idea.

The school principal told the class, “You can use the courtyard outside.”

“My grandma wants to help us,” Gabe told Mrs. Lee. “She has a super garden.”

Gabe's grandma came to school and showed the first graders how to plan their garden.

"We can grow peas and carrots, radishes and lettuce from seeds," she said. "And we can get some small flowers, too."

The first graders had a bake sale to raise money for their garden.

Ben bought a cupcake from his sister.

"I'm so happy," Robin told him. "We're going to grow a million flowers!"

The children's parents came to help them get the ground ready.

They dug weeds and raked the dirt. They fed the garden with things to help the plants grow.

"Can we plant our seeds now?" asked Matt.

"Soon," said Gabe's grandma.

One morning in early spring the children began planting their seeds.

"Good luck, seeds," Robin said.

When the days grew warmer, they planted small, leafy marigolds.

"These plants will have flowers soon," Gabe's grandma told them.
"I love flowers," said Lisa, and she watered each one to help it grow.

Soon tiny seedlings sprouted. Each day the small plants grew and grew.

Every recess the first graders saw new things in their garden.

"I saw two ladybugs," said Meg.
"I saw other bugs," said Nick.
"They are eating our peas."

"We want lots of ladybugs in our garden," said Mrs. Lee. "They will eat the insects nibbling our plants."

Some birds and toads visited the garden. They also ate insects.

Nick and Katie put out a dish of water for the birds.

"The water is for the toads, too," said Katie.

One day Matt raced into the room.

"Some fourth graders ran all over our peas!" he cried.

"Perhaps they didn't see it was our garden," Mrs. Lee said, hugging him.

So the children made a big sign:

This is our garden.
Plants and animals live here.
Please be careful.
Thank you.

"Ben knew it was our garden," Robin said. "Was he there, too?"

"Yes," said Matt. "Your brother was there."

The fourth grade teacher saw the sign. He talked to Mrs. Lee.

"I heard what happened," he told his class. "It may have been an accident. But you hurt the first graders and their garden."

After class Ben walked by the first grade garden. Pea vines and flowers lay on the ground.

Robin and Lisa walked up, carrying cans of water.

"I'm not talking to you," Robin told her brother. "You are mean."

"I was wrong. I'm a toad," he said, trying to make his sister smile.

"No, you're not," said Robin. "Toads are nice."

The next morning Ben got to school early. He talked to his friends. By the time the first graders came, the fourth graders had staked up all the pea vines. And they had fixed the flowers, too.

"We're sorry," said Ben. "We tried to fix your garden. Everyone thinks it's a neat place!"

The fourth graders helped the first graders take care of the garden, and they made sure no one else hurt it.

Every day the plants in the garden grew bigger. The children picked some radishes first.

One morning, Gabe's grandma came to see the garden. "You can pick more vegetables today," she said.

They washed some carrots and gave the first one to their pet rabbit, Martha.

"I hope it tastes good," said Gabe.

Martha ate it fast. She sniffed Gabe's fingers looking for another.

Their carrots were good!

One day the garden was full of ripe vegetables.

"Let's have a party," said Mrs. Lee, "and share our harvest with our friends."

The fourth graders came and so did Gabe's grandma.

"These are for you," said Meg, giving her a big bunch of flowers.

"You made a great garden," Ben told his sister.

"I guess we weren't too little after all," said Robin with a big grin.

“Ladybugs are very little. But they help make a garden a special place,” said Gabe’s grandma. “Ladybugs are a garden’s best friends.”

“And so are you, class,” Mrs. Lee said. “You’re my first grade ladybugs.”

The first grade ladybugs picked their vegetables and made a big salad. Everyone thought it was delicious. Especially Martha!

Make Your Own Garden Indoors

You can grow pretty plants indoors from vegetables. Watch them sprout in just a few days!

Having carrots for dinner? Ask an adult to cut off the top inch or two of an uncooked carrot for your garden.

Stand the carrot top in a shallow dish filled with lukewarm water.

Put your dish near a sunny window. Your carrot plant will need sun and water to grow. As the water disappears, add more water to the dish.

You will begin to see fern-like leaves growing from the top of your carrot in just days.

You can grow other plants by placing the tops of these vegetables in a dish of water:

beet turnip radish parsnip

Rather than water, you can grow your vegetable tops in moistened sand, peat moss, or potting mix. Or you can transplant your vegetables from your dish of water to a pot of soil when the leaves are thick. With care, your plants may live for several months. Enjoy watching your indoor garden grow.